WHITE CLAY
and the
GIANT KANGAROOS

Written by CECILIA EGAN

Illustrated by ELIZABETH ALGER

GECKO
BOOKS

GECKO
BOOKS

ISBN 978-0-9803521-1-5
This edition published in 2007
Reprinted 2009, 2012, 2016
Gecko Books
P.O. Box 118
MARLESTON 5033
South Australia

First published in 1996 by Pan Macmillan Australia Pty. Ltd.

Publication copyright: Gecko Books (JP & PW Enterprises Pty. Ltd.)
Story copyright: Cecilia Egan
Printed in China through Asia Pacific Offset

National Library of Australia
Cataloguing-in-publication data available:
398.2450994

FOREWORD

These wonderful legends of the native Australians have been adapted to be read and understood by children. Young ones too, can gain an insight into the rich and complex culture that existed for tens of thousands of years before Europeans landed.

The stories are not intended to be exact replicas of the original tales, but attempt to convey the narrative in a manner to which children can relate.

Titles in this series:

White Clay and the Giant Kangaroos
The Frog Who Wouldn't Laugh
The Willy-Willy and the Ant
Magic Colours

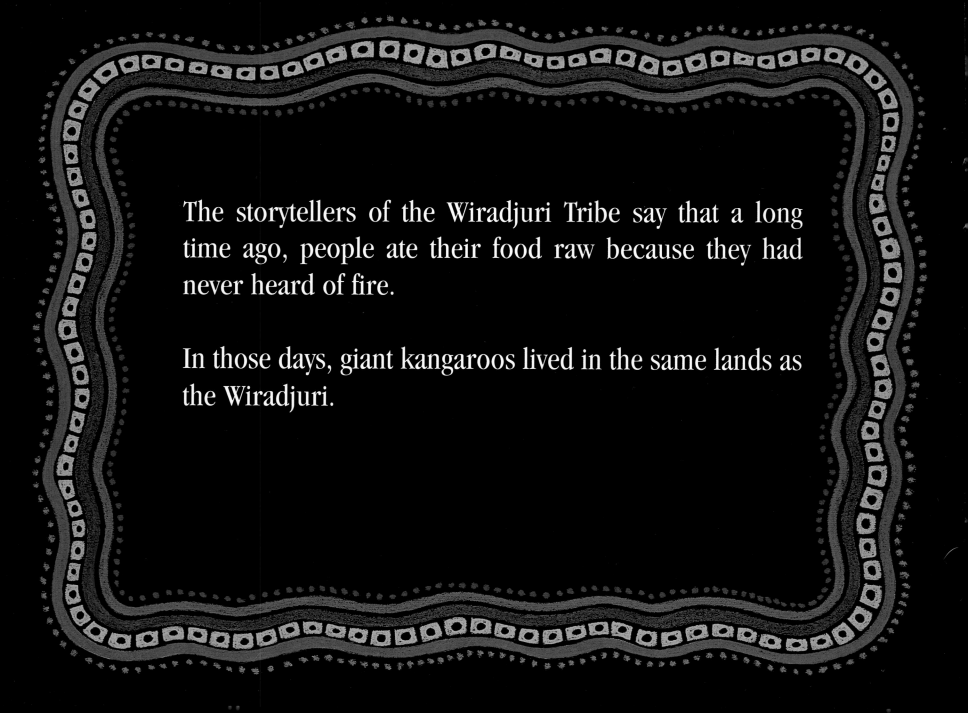

The storytellers of the Wiradjuri Tribe say that a long time ago, people ate their food raw because they had never heard of fire.

In those days, giant kangaroos lived in the same lands as the Wiradjuri.

These kangaroos were three metres tall! That means, if one was in your bedroom it would have to bend over or else its head would hit the ceiling.

The giants ate grass and leaves but they did not like people and sometimes squashed them.

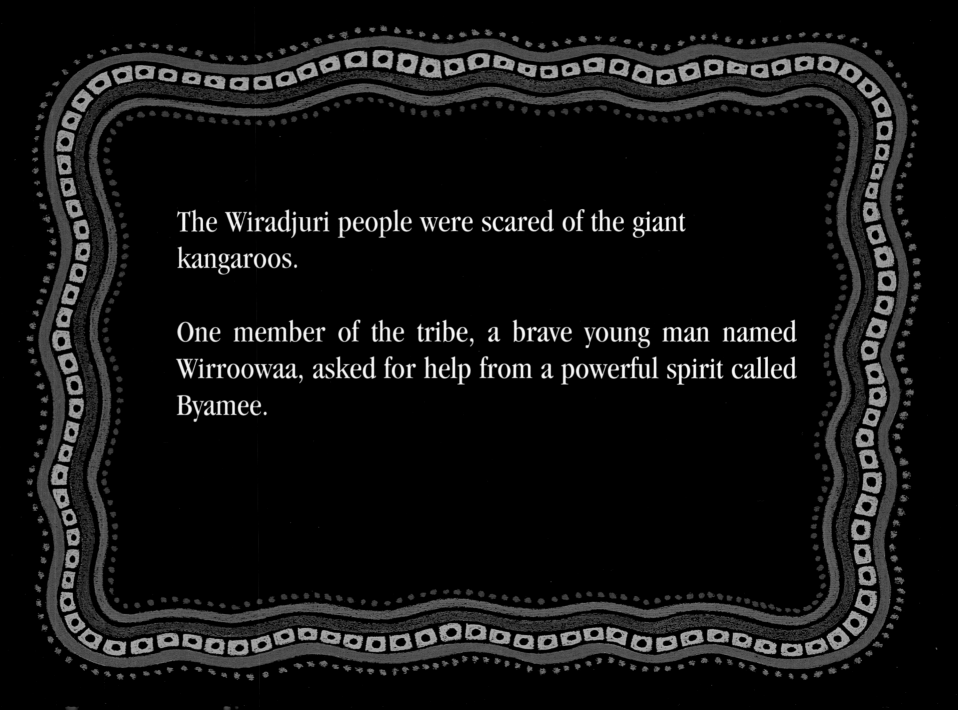

The Wiradjuri people were scared of the giant kangaroos.

One member of the tribe, a brave young man named Wirroowaa, asked for help from a powerful spirit called Byamee.

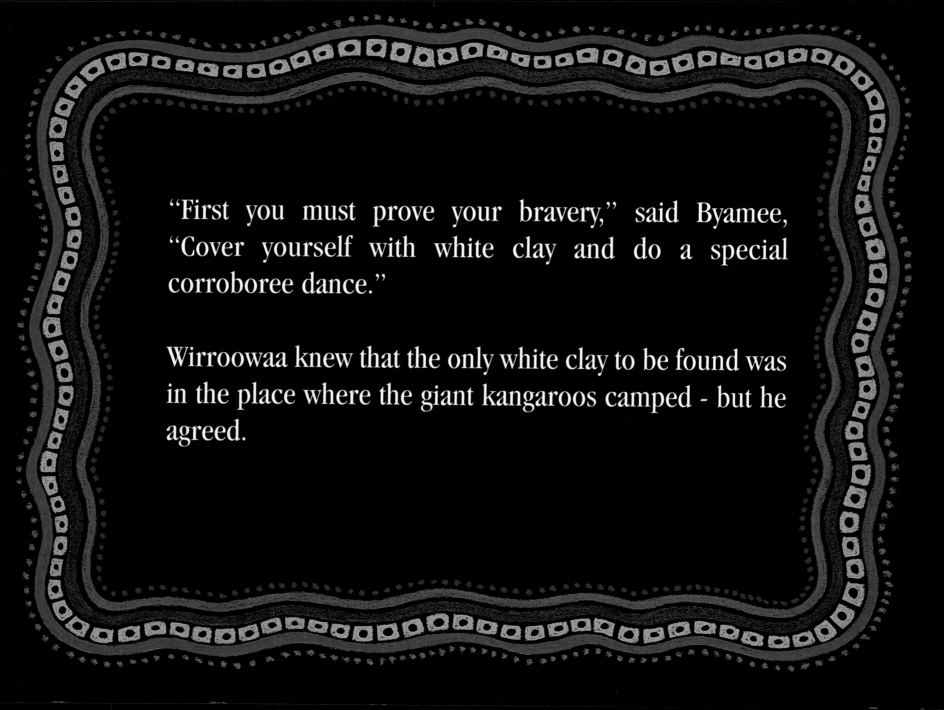

"First you must prove your bravery," said Byamee, "Cover yourself with white clay and do a special corroboree dance."

Wirroowaa knew that the only white clay to be found was in the place where the giant kangaroos camped - but he agreed.

Before he set out to get the white clay, he rubbed goanna fat all over his body, then rolled in the dust until he looked like an ordinary piece of dirt.

Holding a leafy branch in front of him he crept towards the kangaroos' camp.

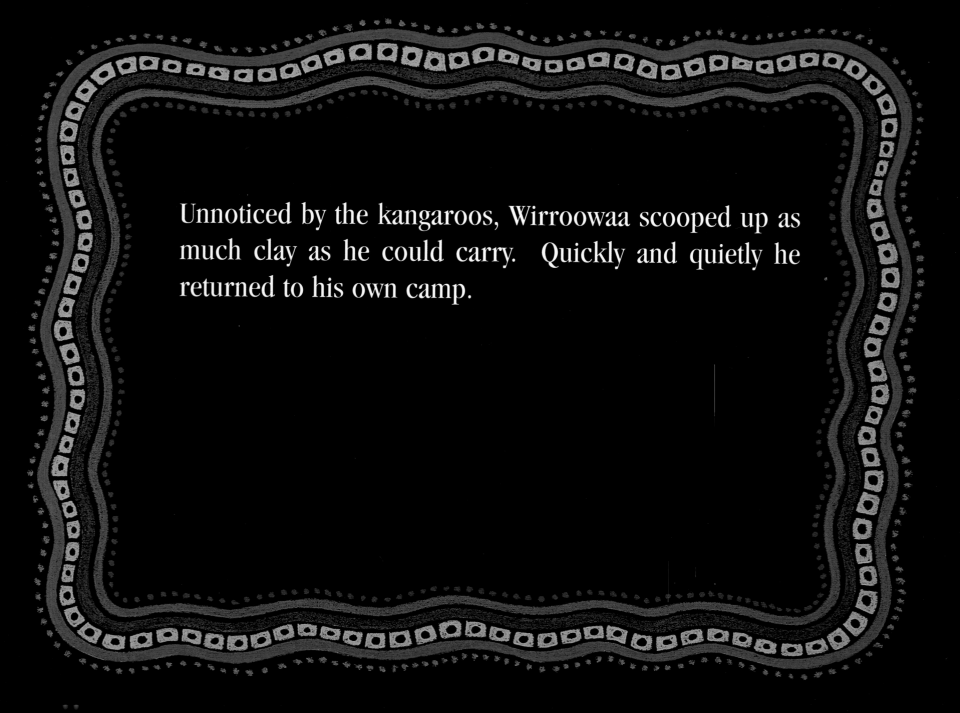

Unnoticed by the kangaroos, Wirroowaa scooped up as much clay as he could carry. Quickly and quietly he returned to his own camp.

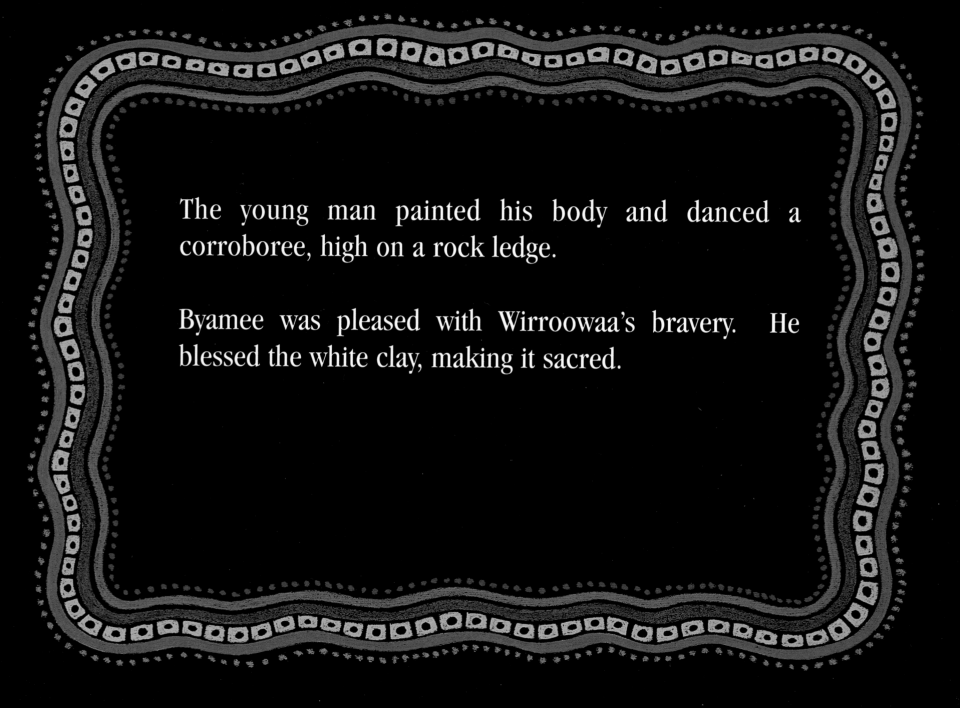

The young man painted his body and danced a corroboree, high on a rock ledge.

Byamee was pleased with Wirroowaa's bravery. He blessed the white clay, making it sacred.

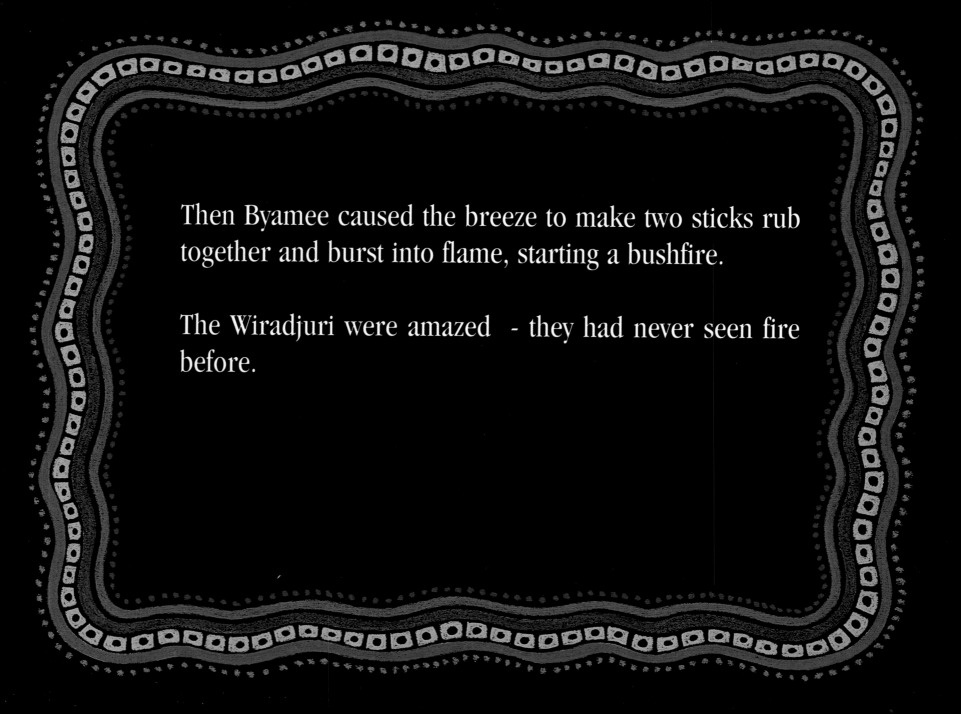

Then Byamee caused the breeze to make two sticks rub together and burst into flame, starting a bushfire.

The Wiradjuri were amazed - they had never seen fire before.

Safe on the rock ledge with Wirroowaa, the tribe watched as the bushfire chased away the kangaroos.

The giant animals never returned.

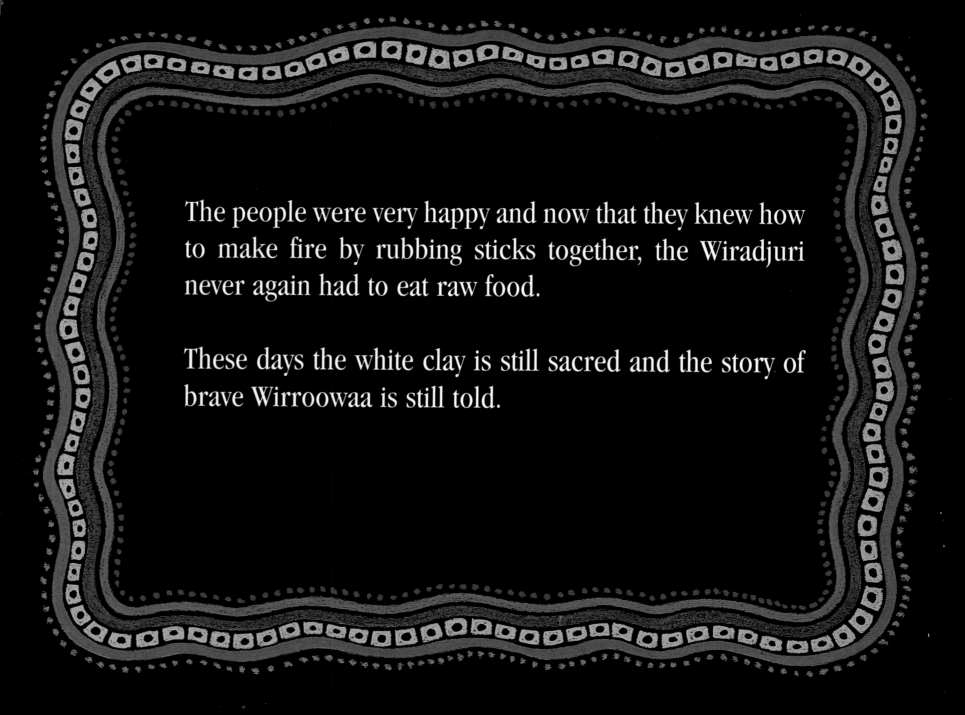

The people were very happy and now that they knew how to make fire by rubbing sticks together, the Wiradjuri never again had to eat raw food.

These days the white clay is still sacred and the story of brave Wirroowaa is still told.